THE LARK

AN EVE OF LIGHT SHORT STORY

HARAMBEE K. GREY-SUN

HYPERVERSE BOOKS, LLC

ALSO BY HARAMBEE K. GREY-SUN

BY HARAMBEE GREY-SUN

Poetry

Spring's Fall (Autumn Numbers * Book I)

Wine Songs, Vinegar Verses

Cover design by The Cover Collection.

Print ISBN-13: 978-1-64044-906-0

Ebook ISBN-13: 978-0-9892661-6-1

Published by **HyperVerse Books, LLC**

www.hyperversebooks.com

writing between and beyond the lines

THE LARK

The plane landed around 11:50 pm. Danny had been promised the car rental booth would close at 12:30 am. She ran through the little two-story airport as fast as her legs could carry her, all 145 pounds of her and her duffle bag, down a frozen escalator and through an automatic door that refused to open automatically. She reached the rental desk at 11:59.

Closed.

Fantastic.

She'd come all the way from Houston to Who-the-Hell-Cared-Where, Pennsylvania to meet up with some no-names who'd posted a classified for singer who had a unique voice and was willing to travel off the beaten path. This was not a promising start.

It was the middle of wherever, but the gig promised to pay quite well—better than a weekend spent bartending, anyway. And the man on the other side of the phone had sounded sincere. But near-desperation could filter all sorts of sounds one didn't want to hear on a cell phone—static, background traffic, snickering . . .

The airport had damn near been sucked dry of sound. Behind her, the luggage turnstile crept with a scratchy whisper as her fellow passengers silently retrieved their bags. She trudged over and eased herself onto a bench, watching for her two bags but more closely observing the twelve, sizing them up, wondering about the type of folks who would come to such an area.

Surely none of them were here on business—though one had claimed otherwise. He'd tried to make conversation with her on the plane, insisting her was a producer coming out this way to look for "lost-and-unfound" talent because he'd heard rumors . . . She thought it curious anyone would come out this way looking for any kind of talent, and she quickly grew suspicious when she realized the guy only introduced himself as being in the music biz after she'd introduced herself as a singer. She'd tuned the guy out for the remainder of the trip.

Presently, she got a better look at him and the others. Even late-night travelers didn't dress in such a patchwork fashion. Many of their shirts seemed to be flannel, but none featured a single distinct color she could name. Their slacks looked like paper bags sewn together, and their shoes didn't appear practical for anything other than standing still. Through lazy lids, the more she regarded them and their sullen expressions, the less they appeared human to her. They were more like rejects from something—products of a broken mold, still unwisely being used. But that was just exhaustion blowing nonsense into her head. Exhaustion and frustration.

This was her first time traveling outside of the southwest. Even at the ripe old age of thirty-two, there was so much she didn't know about the various cultures existing inside the Brave Not-So-New World of the United States.

But she was intelligent enough to know, if not always acknowledge, that each region had its own style. Perfectly normal within a limited radius.

She leaned back and allowed her eyelids to relax completely. This was going to be her first important gig in months, and she probably wouldn't be in any shape to perform. Not on just a few hours of sleep. What was she thinking agreeing to do a breakfast performance, singing in the background at some gathering of farmers, a gathering where the audience would surely be more engrossed in their biscuits and gravy than her voice? Yeah, she was thinking of rent money—but what were the possibilities for any meaningful exposure? The guy who'd auditioned her over the phone just two days prior claimed she was exactly what they needed—a Tex-Mex songstress with a voice more rasp than honey—and he seemed happy enough to send her a plane ticket. At that point, she wasn't going to argue about the arrival time, nor think twice about the two layovers she would have to endure before getting here.

Her eyelids fluttered open, piqued by the realization of complete silence. The turnstile had stopped turning. The claim area was empty. And there was no sign of any abandoned luggage. She stood, glumly looking all about her. *Great.* On top of everything else, she'd a lost bag. And, of course, the service office was closed, its workers undoubtedly as long gone as the car rental folks. Luckily, if not happily, she'd packed all her essentials in her clunky carryon. Deodorant, comb, clean undergarments . . . She hoped the breakfast audience would be more concerned about the appearance of their eggs and flapjacks than of her.

No sense in speculating. Her immediate worry was finding a place to lay her head, preferably near a source of clean water she could use to freshen up afterward, even if she only had time to splash it on her face and pits. Empty or not, she was in an airport. There had to be at least one hotel within walking distance, even in a weird country town.

She exited through the glass doors and crossed the pickup lane. There was nothing beyond the parking lot. No sign of a hotel, motel, or even a shack promising a cheap bed and breakfast. Nothing but darkness and some darker hint of trees far on the horizon.

The parking lot was just as vacant. Her fellow passengers' rides must've arrived before the plane landed, ready to pick up as soon as they exited the building. Final landing of the day, the airport staff had all apparently taken off as well.

Well, maybe not all of them . . . She spotted a white van in the farthest corner of the lot. Bright white, as if it were covered in a layer of fresh snow. Its windows were as black as a snowman's coal eyes. The impression of snow in the middle of June . . . Something was off, and she trusted her intuition.

Someone was still around, maybe close by. Maybe in the vehicle, preparing to start it up, ready to leave. But there'd be no approaching the vehicle, asking for a lift. She knew her horror movie scenarios. She backed up a few steps before doing a one-eighty back through the glass doors. Best to stay in a well-lit building.

She snatched up a map as she passed by the car rental desk, wondering just why all of the airport's lights were still on and all the doors unlocked, as if it were just past noon rather than just past midnight.

She picked up the desk's blue phone while gazing at the cab advertisements on the back of the folded map. No dial tone. She figured it was too much to ask that everything be working at this hour. Anyway, calling at this point seemed far more trouble than it was worth: Trying to stay awake while the cab arrived, then trusting it to take her to a decent motel without running up the meter . . . She'd have been more inclined if she could trust her smartphone to stay up with her through all that, but she'd realized when boarding the plane that her phone was almost out of juice. Turning it on now and keeping it on until the cab arrived would kill it. Of course, she'd had the brilliant foresight to pack the charger with the other nonessentials in her lost luggage.

She left the desk, unfolding the map as she wandered. It seemed she hadn't been too far off considering this area the middle of wherever. The map showed only the airport at its center with nothing but an open field surrounding it. At the far edges were the trees she thought she'd made out in the dark. The map had no scale or anything else useful to determine the distance from the airport to the trees. It didn't matter to her. In the morning, she'd be driving through it, not walking it—even if the map oddly showed no roads or paths.

She looked up from the map and spotted a ladies' room. No sense in waiting till sunrise to wash travel's grime off her face. Something also had to be done with what was left of her late-night burger and fries. She checked three stalls before finding one with toilet paper, hung her bag on the door's hook, and then sat down with a sigh.

She'd get some shuteye on the bench in the baggage claim area. It was barely even comfortable to sit on, but when the car rental desk opened at six, she'd be in a prime position to get what she needed and get the hell out of there. Her performance started at eight; the location she'd been given surely couldn't be that far away.

She sighed again as she wiped and pulled up her jeans. She'd a funny feeling in her stomach. It never failed. Dropping a little load always made her a little hungry. During her earlier mad dash, she'd noticed a vending machine upstairs, one containing nuts and dried fruit in addition to the usual cavity creators; she'd swing by on her way to the bench. She flushed, grabbed her bag, and opened the stall door.

A man stood mere feet away, staring back at her.

Her shriek created some distance, as if her voice had arms that shoved him back a few feet while also causing her to stumble backward. She caught herself before falling onto the toilet.

Whatever had caused him to retreat a few steps, the grizzled man appeared in no way frightened. He wore a stained, gray jumpsuit and tattered ball cap; his eyes were bloodshot and his hands were scarred many times over. He'd clearly experienced plenty of frightening things in his time. His sun-ravaged skin gave her the impression of vet from a long ago war, or maybe a long one still going.

"Ex-excuse me." She wanted to rush past him, but she lacked the energy for such a burst. Fear didn't jolt her; it nearly paralyzed her.

The man said nothing as the right side of his upper lip curled—a wavering snarl probably deciding whether to growl or curse at her.

She couldn't run, but she could talk. "Ar-are you lost?" She could ask stupid questions. Of course the old creep didn't belong in the ladies' room.

The man didn't take his eyes off her, and didn't stop snarling, as he reached into his back pocket.

Danny edged forward out of the stall, now ready to attempt to bolt if this crazy pulled out a knife. Fear was being eclipsed by a need to survive.

The man had no blade, at least not one that he flashed, but an orange badge. He held it up, stomach high. Danny glanced down and saw his picture, a name she couldn't pronounce, and a word she could. *Maintenance.*

Of course. The janitor. That had to be his van outside.

She nodded—almost bowed—and forced a wry smile. "Sorry. I'll get out of your way."

The man didn't move as she stepped toward the exit. He only turned his head, letting his eyes follow her out.

She breathed relief upon reaching the hall, as if someone who'd been holding a pillow on her face for a full minute had finally let go. She hurried on in some direction, just away from the bathroom, shoving herself through the dead automatic door, casting glances over her shoulders all the while until she was confident the man wasn't creeping after her.

She almost tripped on the first step of the escalator. Catching herself, she tried to regain her breath as she took one last good look behind her.

Still no sign of a pursuer. Also no sign of any cleaning supplies.

Shit.

Exiting the bathroom, she saw no cart with janitorial equipment, no mop-and-bucket, not even so much as a broom or dustpan. Her heart rate increased as her breathing again got away from her. Those meditation classes she'd taken last fall hadn't done much good; she could rarely control her breath when it mattered most. Out-of-control breathing led to out-of-control thinking.

After a few panicking minutes, she managed to consider that "maintenance" didn't necessarily mean "janitor." Maybe the guy was in there to fix something—a clogged sink, perhaps. She hadn't gotten the chance to use one, never even glanced toward the row of sinks after she'd flushed. Maybe his tools had been there.

She walked up the escalator, motivated not by a fear satiated, but by a hunger that had yet to be. She started toward the area where she remembered seeing the vending machines when something caught her eye that she hadn't noticed before: Three small kiosks that—during normal business hours—sold cookies, pretzels, and cheap trinkets, respectively.

As she stared, the odors of chocolate and peanut butter quickened her. She wasn't on a diet—what did she need with nuts or dried fruit from a vending machine? A packaged candy bar that may've been sitting in the machine for six months was easy to resist, but one-day-old or even two-day-old cookies would take a will stronger than a mortal woman's.

But she surprised herself. She wasn't completely at the mercy of the butterflying pangs in her stomach. Eying the kiosks, she convinced herself that she'd easier tolerate a pretzel than one or two cookies. She could never enjoy cookies without milk; the water fountain would do for a salty pretzel. Anyway, the cookies were more heavily guarded.

All three kiosks were in cages, but the cages were loose and flimsy. With enough strength and effort, she could pry one open enough to wedge herself inside. When she checked the cage for the pretzel stand, however, it slid right open. The lock wasn't loose. It had been broken.

She slid on through and put her hands on the glass counter, preparing to hoist herself over. Then she heard it.

It sounded almost like a squeak—two of them. It wasn't her hands. She froze, concentrating on any sound entering her ears. She heard *chittering*. It was coming from behind the counter.

She peered over. Huddled in a ball and staring back at

her was a skinny, ill-clad teenage girl. She was clearly trying to make herself as small as possible, like a frightened cat, but she made no attempt to cover her head or shut her wide-open eyes when Danny spotted her.

Those eyes . . . They seemed all pupil, covered with a thin, bluish translucent film. Some kind of disorder—was the girl blind?

"What are you doing?" Danny asked.

The girl said nothing, only stared.

Danny began again: "Are you—?"

The girl interrupted. "Help. Me. Serve. Hive. Them."

The girl physically appeared to be at least sixteen years old, but she spoke with the voice of someone at least half that age, and with a manner of someone plagued with hiccups. Mentally *and* physically disabled. She appeared malnourished and wore ill-fitting clothes and a few of the trinkets from the adjacent kiosk. Her face was smudged and her mousy brown hair looked like a real mouse had run through it. There were dark spots under her eyes —*Those eyes . . .*

"Who are you hiding from?" Danny whispered. "Who's after you?"

"Know. One," the girl said.

No one? "But you just—" Danny stopped herself. The girl clearly wasn't right in the head, but she was lost, or abandoned. Possibly a runaway. Whichever, she needed help only someone answering 911 could provide.

Danny heaved herself over the counter and crouched, leaning closer to the girl. "I'm going to call for help, okay?" She turned on her cell phone. "You'll be safe soon." No signal. *Damn.* "We're going to have to get from out of here." She began to stand when the girl grabbed at her sleeve.

"Knot. Time."

"What? We have to get the *police* out here." Danny glanced at her phone. "We have to—" She stopped and stared at her phone. The display read 3:55 am.

She hadn't been in the airport for more than thirty minutes, forty-five at most. Was her phone broken, picking up a weird signal? Or had she actually fallen asleep in the baggage claim?

She crouched down again. "Listen. My phone is on its last legs, and I can't get a good signal in here. We have to go outside. I need to get you some proper help."

"Knot. Time. Sun. Wait."

The girl clearly wasn't in full grasp of her situation, and Danny couldn't think of a way to convince her. The fact she was a teenager was bad enough—since hitting her late twenties, Danny had always had a problem relating to anyone not old enough to legally drink—but the fact that the girl's mind was much younger than her body made it even worse. Danny had no kids of her own, and wouldn't know what to do with them if she had, just like she didn't know what to do now. Should she leave the kid here, go outside to make the call, and then return?

She stood up. She needed to get the circulation going in her legs. While stretching, she looked around for the nearest exit—instead, she saw a figure cresting the escalator. The maintenance man.

She shook her head, quietly cursing herself for not thinking of it immediately. The girl was hiding from the old man. She may've been his daughter, she may've been a kidnap victim. At the moment, it didn't matter. Danny had only two thoughts: the old bastard was the abusive sort and the girl had to be kept away from him at all costs.

The man stopped when he stepped on the floor, and made eye contact.

"C'mon!" Danny grabbed the girl by the elbow; she pulled her up with such ease it was as if she didn't even have bones.

She tugged the girl along as she slid out of the cage and headed in the opposite direction from the man who, as far as Danny could tell, wasn't hurrying after them. That was fortunate. With both duffel bag and girl in tow, she couldn't do much more than trot like a crippled dog.

They had to get downstairs. The only working exit she knew was downstairs. And the only stairs she knew were the escalators. The door by which she entered after deplaning would of course be locked, but a frantic mind pushed her in that direction anyway as she kept an eye out for any emergency exits.

After deplaning on the runway, she and the other passengers had to climb a metal staircase and enter the airport on the upper level, where all the terminals were. The blue door, as she suspected, was now locked, as were the blue doors in the other four terminals she checked. The old man hadn't caught up to them—at least Danny didn't hear or see him—but she still felt trapped. She'd seen no red signs, no emergency exits. They'd have to make their way back toward the escalator, back toward him.

"You? Range? El?"

They were the first words the girl had spoken since they'd left the kiosk, and they were even more puzzling than her previous words.

"No," was all Danny could think to say, as she turned on her phone. She hoped to get a signal near the windows. She wasn't quite sure what the girl was asking, but she figured she had an answer as good as any. "My name's Danny."

"Like? Me? Speh? Shell?"

Poor thing. The girl was special all right, but Danny

wondered what made her think there was a connection between them. Her phone showed no signal; it only displayed the time. 4:15 am. "I'm nothing special," Danny said with a sigh. "Just a tired singer short on luck."

The girl grinned at her. "Sing. Her." Her teeth appeared as if she'd been fed a steady diet of rocks. That may've accounted for the chittering sound the girl sometimes made. Danny hoped, once rescued, the girl would be whisked off to an oral surgeon, in addition to other medical specialists.

"C'mon," Danny said, "we have to keep going. Do I still need to drag you, or do you promise to follow?"

The girl nodded with a grin.

Danny released her arm and gestured. "Let's go. If I shout 'run,' you run. Okay?"

The girl nodded again.

With her staccato manner of speaking and odd reactions, Danny wasn't sure how much the girl really understood. She also wasn't sure how effectively the girl could run with those pencil-thin legs and wobbling knees.

They proceeded with more caution this time, Danny's thoughts darting as quickly as her eyes. She again saw the vending machines. Next to them, she saw a faded orange door, unmarked. She hadn't noticed it before, no doubt due to its dingy color; it was almost of a piece with the walls. In normal circumstances, she would leave well enough alone. At the moment, she was willing to check any door not marked "Sudden Death." She gestured, and the girl followed close.

It was unlocked; a dim light shone from somewhere behind it. Danny slowly pushed the door open, wary that someone might be on the other side. She heard nothing, so she pushed it all the way, venturing a step forward. The door opened up onto a balcony. She stepped all the way in, moved all the way forward to peer over the railing.

Below were rows and piles of luggage. Suitcases, duffle bags, guitar bags, suitbags—almost every sort of traveling bag she could imagine. Some, closer to the room's edges, were lined up or stacked neatly on top of one another. Closer to the center were large mounds of bags, carelessly tossed.

There were hundreds. Several hundred. Danny wondered to whom they could possibly belong. Surely it couldn't have all been lost luggage? She scanned the area more closely, as well as the dim light and distance would permit. She thought she spotted her own red bag near a door, among the bags neatly lined up. If only she knew where the other side of that door was and could get down there and check . . .

She heard the girl chittering behind her. Danny regarded her and remembered. *Priorities.* They had to get outside first.

She closed the door and gestured for the girl to follow her as before. They continued on slowly, and slowed even more when the kiosks came into sight. The old creep had to be hiding behind one of them, maybe hiding *in* one of them, waiting to spring once she and the girl passed. Surely, he had the key to the cages. He probably had a key to everything that could be locked around here.

Danny moved closer to the wall and reached out, placing a hand on the girl's shoulder as they inched by, her sight glued to the kiosks, the pretzel one in particular. She remembered how she'd seen no sign of the hiding girl until she almost jumped on the poor thing. She wouldn't take her eyes off the kiosks, not until she reached the escalators.

The girl chittered. Danny looked and saw the girl was

staring at something behind her. She turned. They were right next to the escalator. The old man was standing on the top step, two paces away, staring right back.

Danny shrieked, and the man wavered. Without thinking, she unslung her bag and heaved it toward his head while shouting, "Run!"

Not waiting to see if the old man was hit, or even whether the girl had started running on her own, Danny grabbed her by the wrist and hustled down the other escalator, ignoring the protesting sounds from the girl she was trying to protect. As they approached the automatic door, she was ready to push through but, to her surprise, she found it working. They didn't slow pace until they reached the glass-door exit in the baggage claim area. Danny hesitated but kept moving, barging into them. They were still unlocked. *Thank God.*

"Stop," the girl said. "*Stop!*"

Danny halted, panting. She looked at the girl, glanced toward the glass doors behind them, and then at the girl again.

"Hurt." The girl said the word, but made no gesture to indicate just where she was hurting. She only stood looking back toward the glass doors.

Danny tried to catch her breath. "S-sorry." As frazzled as she felt, she imagined the girl felt worse. She wanted to say that she was just trying to save her from further abuse, but for all she knew just saying the word or anything close would cause the girl to vividly remember the episodes. The girl was already upset; no need to upset her further. And no need for them to remain strangers.

"What's your name?" Danny asked.

The girl turned to her. She nodded as she spoke. "Knell. Uh."

Danny smiled. "That's cute. Don't worry, Nella." She pulled her phone out of her pocket and turned it on. "We'll be in happy land soon enough."

Reception—*finally*.

Danny kept her eyes on the glass doors as she dialed.

"Nine-one-one. What's your emergency?"

"Kidnapping! Child abu—" She took a breath. "Please just get the police out here now!"

"Okay, ma'am, calm down. Where are you calling from?"

"The airport. I'm at the airport."

"Which one?"

"I—" Danny didn't know. She patted her pockets. It had to be on her boarding pass, or on the map she'd picked up from the car rental desk . . . the map she'd stuffed into her bag, along with the boarding pass she'd stuffed in there when she'd originally boarded. *Shit.*

She looked around frantically for a sign, but saw nothing. She'd have to go back inside to grab another map.

"Ma'am? Ma'am, where are you? Which airport?"

"I'll tell you in a second. Hold on." Danny pantomimed for Nella to stay put as she started toward the doors. She'd run in, grab another map, and run right back out.

She got three steps before she saw him standing there, staring her down. Hanging over his left arm and shoulder was what appeared to be a rolled hose.

"Ma'am? What—?"

Her phone cut off. Dead.

She dropped it and spun around, reaching for Nella. She grabbed the girl's arm and started forward, in the general direction of the white van. When the van's bright headlights flicked on, she froze. Stark fear . . . paralyzed . . .

Danny could only remember how Nella first told her —*asked* her—to help her survive "them."

"Them" undoubtedly had her and Nella outnumbered, overpowered. Only wits would save the two of them. That, or a miracle.

It was a fool's hope but, pulling Nella with her, Danny headed into the field. A van didn't have to stay on the road, but she hoped there were some rocks or large branches or something otherwise that would make the terrain uneven and thus difficult for the vehicle. The maintenance man was slow. And even though he was a man, Danny figured she could hold her own in a confrontation, long enough at least for Nella to scramble away if she had sense enough to.

They'd gone a good distance, maybe even half a mile, before Danny's desire for uneven terrain backfired. She was nimble enough to let go of Nella before falling on her face, but she wasn't so quick to recover. She figured there'd be branches and rocks and potholes, but Danny had tripped over something as large as a log. She sat up, catching her breath while getting her bearings.

The van's lights were still on. She could see them in the far distance. It hadn't moved from the parking lot. There was no sign of the old man, either. She heard nothing other than her own breathing, her own heart rate—and Nella, chittering.

The girl needed help, more help than she was capable of giving. Danny still couldn't help but ask, "Are you alright?"

The only response was something hard and metallic slamming against the back of Danny's head.

DANNY KNEW the sun had risen before she even opened her eyes. She felt the early morning chill, the dew on her skin—

all *over* her skin. She regretted the new day, more so when her eyelids parted.

She was still in the same field. She instinctively knew she was lying next to the object she'd tripped over before blacking out. She was facing its face—the face of one of the passengers who'd been on the plane with her. The record producer.

His eyes bugged out. His mouth hung open for a scream that would never come. His tongue protruded, touching the grass.

Danny supported herself on a shoulder and elbow, shooting daggers throughout her nervous system as she pushed up and got a better view of the man. Like her, he'd been stripped naked. Unlike her, he'd been eviscerated. His entrails were inches away from her fingers.

She scrambled, backing away while trying to stand without touching any part of the butchery. She was on her buttocks but couldn't get to her feet before backing into something else. Her fingers felt something glutinous before she saw it. Although groggy, her mind was quick enough to grasp what it might be. Another passenger from her flight: denuded and disemboweled.

She shrieked as she forced herself to a standing position. Then, she didn't dare move.

Everyone who'd flown to this hellhole with her now surrounded her. All were massacred, mutilated. All of them except her. She alone . . . She—alone with the two other living figures standing just beyond the mass of bodies. The old man and Nella. Side by side.

The girl was naked but didn't seem at all bothered by the morning chill. A noose had been tied around her neck, undoubtedly by the old man. He held the other end, wrapped around his left arm and shoulder. The "hose"

Danny had seen was more accurately some kind of cord. The man grasped a blue metallic rod in his other hand. It looked almost like an aluminum baseball bat, but it was about five feet long. Most likely it was the item that had knocked her cold. He raised it slightly as he stepped forward. Nella remained where she stood.

The old man avoided bodies and entrails without looking down even once. His eyes were focused on Danny's. She wanted to look away—she wanted *run* away—but she'd no will to move. She stayed put until the man stopped a few paces in front of her.

"Time for breakfast." The man spoke with a voice that made him sound twice as old as he looked. "Sing."

Danny was aghast.

"Sing." The man leveled the metal rod, pointing it just under her ribs, and jabbed. Danny felt the pain spiral several inches from the point of impact. She wanted to vomit.

"Sing."

The man kept jabbing her—in the ribs, under the ribs, in the sternum—while commanding her, gazing into her eyes without a single blink.

Danny didn't vomit. The prodding rapidly became less painful. Her midsection had gone numb.

She hadn't been exactly clear-headed when she awoke, and she was getting foggier with each passing moment. The man's eyes seemed to glow a luminescent yellow before flashing red, like emergency lights. Whether real or halluci-nated, the flashes and the prodding pumped her insides. Her vessels and cords thrummed while something that had been dammed back prepared for its release.

She no longer had a choice. A poisonous frisson over-took her, as if her insides were being hurried over by millions of fiery insects. She opened her mouth wide, then let loose.

It started as possibly the most ungodly scream ever heard. The old man stumbled backward several feet at its force, falling backward over a corpse but without loosening his grip on either the rod or the cord. Danny's high-pitched scream lasted only a few seconds before descending into a powerful melody. It was then that Nella began to move. The girl didn't fall backward: She shook as if in the throes of an epileptic fit.

Danny wanted to run to her, but she couldn't move. She could only sing, and she couldn't stop.

She sang one long uninterrupted song through a range of styles, including the warbling style that had won her a loyal but small following in the Houston area—the same style that had won over the mysterious man on the other side of the phone just a few days prior.

She thought little now about whom that man could've been—it certainly wasn't the old man. Nella occupied her thoughts now. Nella, whose skin ripped open as the girl seized up and thrashed about. Nella, whose bones snapped and broke, to jut through the skin and reshape her arms and legs. Nella, whose jaw and face deformed itself. Nella, whose multiplying streams of blood sparkled like rivulets of crimson glitter.

Danny couldn't shut her eyes, couldn't shut out the sight of Nella spasmodically dancing to her song—leaping, tumbling to the ground, hopping, scratching, leaping into the air again—as her body changed, transmogrified into something with claws . . . with a beak . . . with arms twisted and pulled back behind her like a V.

The noose about her neck served its purpose. The old man had returned to his feet, caring nothing about Danny as he minded Nella and the cord. It was like a leash, made of material the girl couldn't break even as she grew wilder, clearly stronger, and less recognizably human. The rising sun appeared to lend support to the grotesque spectacle. In Danny's eyes, the sun's rays filtered into visible but free-floating strings in the girl's presence, jittering strings of nameless colors. Intentionally or not, the strings caught on the blood and stuck. They became more complex and took on patterns, as more accumulated.

Danny tried to push her song into another horrific scream. Instead, her voice simply switched into another melody as she witnessed what was once a frail, bruised girl complete her transformation into a large bird of broken flesh, fresh blood, light and shadow.

The creature was as tall as Nella had been, between five and six feet, but that was the only similarity. It still seemed to be in the middle of a fit as it flexed and fluttered its bright wings, feathers of light draping down her twisted, bony, bent-back arms. It perhaps would've flown away if not for the strong cord and impressive strength of the old man. He held the unruly cord with one hand as he grasped his rod in the other.

The creature flew up several feet and then fluttered down, landing near one of the mutilated bodies. It pecked among the innards until it caught the intestines in its beak. It wrestled with the entrails as if they were a living worm before managing to swallow them whole. It then picked and chose from among the other spillage before pecking at its own body and taking an abbreviated flight, alighting next to another corpse.

If only Danny could shut her eyes, shut her mouth, stitch them both shut . . . This was all some sort of devilish magic, something abominable that was somehow in some way being aided by her voice and possibly her very witness. But she couldn't shut up. She couldn't shut out the view.

The bird-like creature—Nella at its core—didn't seem quite finished with its transformation. It was beyond human, but the more Danny watched, the more it seemed to be trying to remake itself further. The sun even seemed complicit in the process.

The creature picked at the corpses and also pecked at its own body, rending itself, repairing itself—stitching with the thinnest rays of morning sunlight—dining and dancing, delighted by the song extorted through a torture Danny could never hope to describe with coherent words. And the bodies—the *nobodies*—that were ripped apart . . . What were the proper words for them? What more had they to lose?

Much more, it seemed.

Finished with the flesh, Nella hovered above the twice-over massacre and contributed a birdsong, pinching and altering it until reaching harmony with Danny, who in turn saw incorporeal forms rising from the corpses on the ground—appearing as irradiated insects of all shapes and sizes—floating upward toward Nella. Danny lost count after fifty. Nella then ceased her song and proceeded to snatch and swallow them all.

Breakfast. A feast on pieces of broken flesh and broken souls.

Danny stopped singing and fell to her knees. Though exhausted, she now understood. She understood her role in this black and sunny ritual—not as a singer, but as an instrument. The creature fed on both bodies *and* souls, and it needed the assistance of folks like Danny to live, to *survive*.

There'd be no assistance for Danny. She was through. Used up. She had no words, no pleas, no cries. Her throat was bone-dry.

Perhaps that's why the creature now appeared satiated. It alighted one last time and didn't even regard Danny. It turned its beak into its breast to rest while it molted light, slowly reverting to the form of a sleeping girl. An image from a fairy tale penned in Hell.

Danny's insides had been pushed to mush—nothing fit for a hellfowl. But maybe someone else was hungry . . .

The old man drove his rod into the ground with the strength of one three times his size. He wrapped his end of the cord around the pole, tethering the sleeping Nella to something sturdy lest she wake unexpectedly. He then turned his eyes back to Danny.

Almost totally expunged of anything resembling life, she let the man hoist her up like a sack of oats. He slung her over his shoulder and carried her away from the bodies, toward the green perimeter.

Only her eyes seemed to function. As she got closer, Danny saw it wasn't trees that encircled the meadow. It was a high barricade—a fence or a wall—overpopulated with green bags, each six to seven feet in length. Each one had been stuffed with something and strung up—for who-the-hell-cared what reason. Danny's nervous system could no longer tolerate answers.

The maintenance man carefully laid Danny's numb body on the grass. He stepped out of her range of vision for a few minutes and returned with a green bag draped around his shoulders. For a moment, he stood looking down at her with the same expression he'd worn when she first saw him. He was no janitor. He was a committed soldier of a long and secret war still ongoing.

The old man laid the bag beside Danny and unzipped it. He gently lifted her, and then placed her inside, face-up.

Danny wasn't the most sophisticated woman. There was

so much she didn't know or quite understand about this Brave Not-So-New World of 21st Century America. But she was smart enough to know that her ticket had not been to a town at all. Her real destination had been to some kind of facility. This whole set-up was some elaborate configuration designed to keep that body-and-soul-eater "Nella" alive. This went beyond the girl and the maintenance man. At the end of the day, they too were probably just like her—instruments in someone else's scheme, destined to be food for someone's twisted dream.

Before the zipper closed the bag over her eyes, Danny saw a passenger plane making its final descent. She wondered how many would be entertained for lunch.

ABOUT THE SERIES

Eve of Light is a Dark Metaphysical Fantasy series chronicling the surreal events leading up to the Apocalypse—the Death of God. The setting is a contemporary, alternate Earth on the verge of a cataclysm that will warp space, time, and minds. The main narrative of those plotting and battling to save humanity is told in the *Eve of Light* series of novels. The short stories and novellas are simply flashes on the fringe—episodes told from the perspective of everyday men and women living in a world turned weird.

The Core Novels

BloodLight: The Apocalypse of Robert Goldner
Broken Angels *(Eve of Light * Book I)*
Divinities, Entangled *(Eve of Light * Book II)*

Stories on the Fringe

FoolKillers
The Lark
Heaven's Gun
Knotty & Ice
Rogue Beauty
Deviant-Hunter's Sabbath

ABOUT THE AUTHOR

Harambee K. Grey-Sun writes under the broad umbrella of speculative fiction. He integrates elements of fantasy, horror, noir, black humor, and science fiction into his work and spins dark, surreal, mysterious, grotesque, at times challenging, and often blasphemous tales. Many of his stories can be categorized into one or more of the following subgenres: speculative thriller, urban fantasy, metaphysical fantasy, superhero, occult/supernatural, slipstream, and–*of course*– weird fiction. His Dark Metaphysical Fantasy series *Eve of Light* examines the dark nature of God and what it really means to be human.

For more information:
www.harambeegreysun.com